The Palace Statues

Written by Cynthia Rider
Illustrated by Alex Brychta

OXFORD
UNIVERSITY PRESS

The children put on a play called *The Golden Statue*. Chip was the statue. He had on a golden cloak and gold face paint.

"I like this gold face paint," said Anneena.

The magic key began to glow.

The magic took the children to a palace. They saw a man talking to a girl.

"Don't cry, Eva," he said.

"What's the matter?" asked Biff.

"This is my brother, Aran," said Eva. "He guards the golden statues in the palace."

"The statues all have jewels," said Aran. "But someone is stealing the jewels, and I *must* catch the robber."

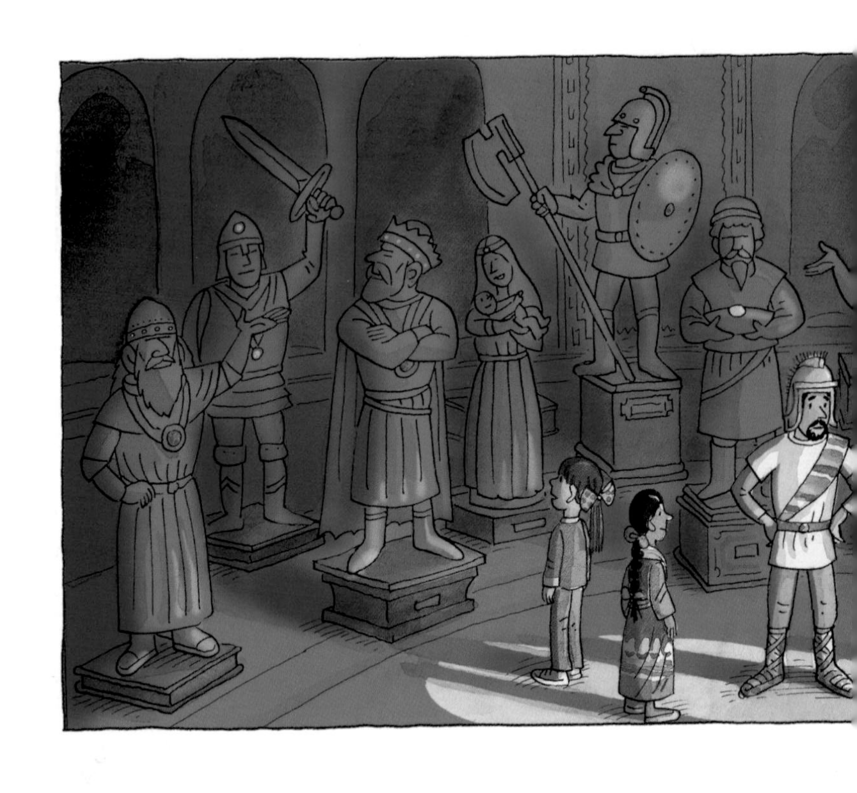

Aran showed the children the golden statues. “The robber might steal more jewels tonight,” he said. “What can I do?”

Chip had an idea. “You can dress up as a golden statue,” he said. “Then you can keep watch.”

That night, Aran dressed up as a golden statue.

"I'm glad we've got this gold face paint," said Anneena.

Aran went into the statue room. He stood in the deepest shadows.

"You need a jewel," said Eva. She gave him her necklace, and went out.

Suddenly, a secret door slid open. Two men crept into the room. They took the rest of the jewels.

One of the men spotted Aran.

"I didn't see that statue last night," he said. "Let's get that necklace."

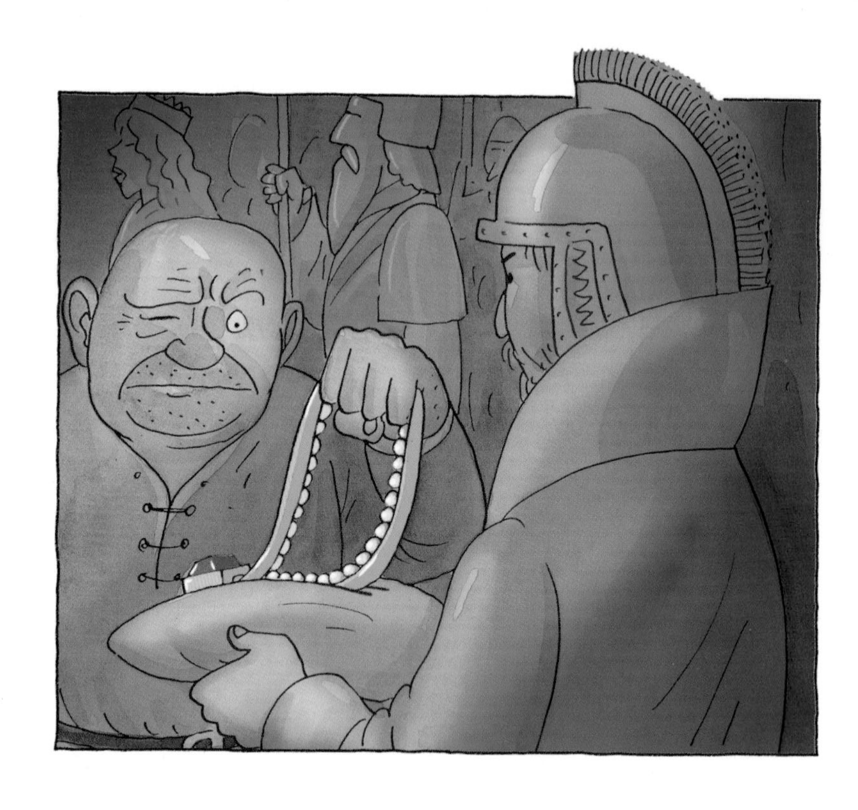

Aran held his breath as the man grabbed the necklace.

At last, he heard a soft thud as the secret door slid shut.

Aran called the children. He showed them the secret door. They all crept down some steps and along a shadowy tunnel.

Suddenly, Biff tripped and fell.

"Who's there?" shouted the men.

"Run!" whispered Nadim. "Hide under the steps."

A robber came up to the steps. He held up his lamp but the children were as still as statues.

"There's nobody here," he said.

The men went into a dusty room. The children followed them and peeped round the door.

“There’s another door!” said Aran. “It must lead into the palace garden. They might escape through that.”

“I know what we can do,” said Nadim, and he told the others his plan.

“That’s a good idea,” said Eva.

Eva raced back up the steps. She told the guards to go to the garden door. Then she ran back to the others.

Aran marched stiffly into the dusty room.

"Give me back my necklace!" he roared, in a voice like thunder.

The robbers jumped up.

"Help! The statue is alive!" they screamed. They raced out of the garden door . . .

. . . and ran right into the guards!

The next day, Aran and Eva gave the children a golden statue.

"Thank you for helping us," they said. The magic key began to glow.

The magic took the children home.

"The statue looks just like Eva," said Nadim.

"Yes," said Chip. "And Anneena looks just like the statue!"

Think about the story

Why was
Eva crying?

What was
Nadim's plan?

How do you
think the children
felt when they
were hiding?

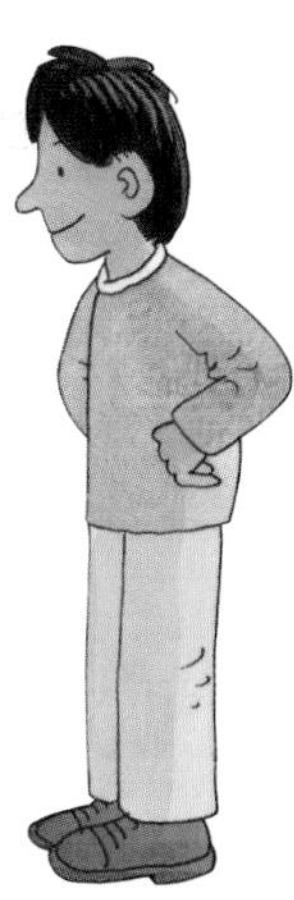

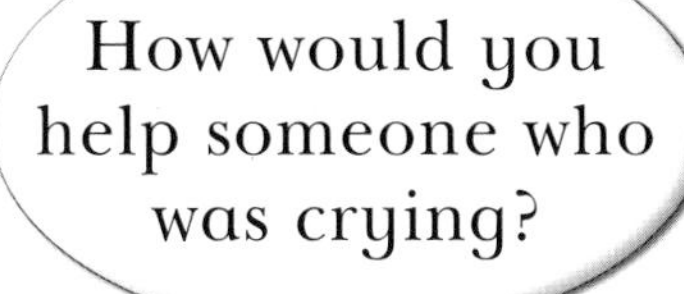

Helping Aran

Help Aran to match the jewels to the statues.

Useful common words repeated in this story and other books in the series.

began called children door face garden gave idea might others room suddenly

Names in this story: Anneena Aran Biff Chip Eva Nadim